Flies and Mosquitoes

Sally Cowan

Contents

What Are Flies and Mosquitoes?

Flies and mosquitoes are flying insects with two wings. There are thousands of different kinds of flies and mosquitoes.

Some common flies include the housefly, the blowfly and the tiny fruit fly. These flies are usually grey or brown with stripes, but some blowflies are shiny blue or green. Flies are mostly active during the day.

housefly

blowfly

Mosquitoes are insects that bite.
Most kinds of mosquitoes are grey or brown.
They are mostly active in the evening and at night.

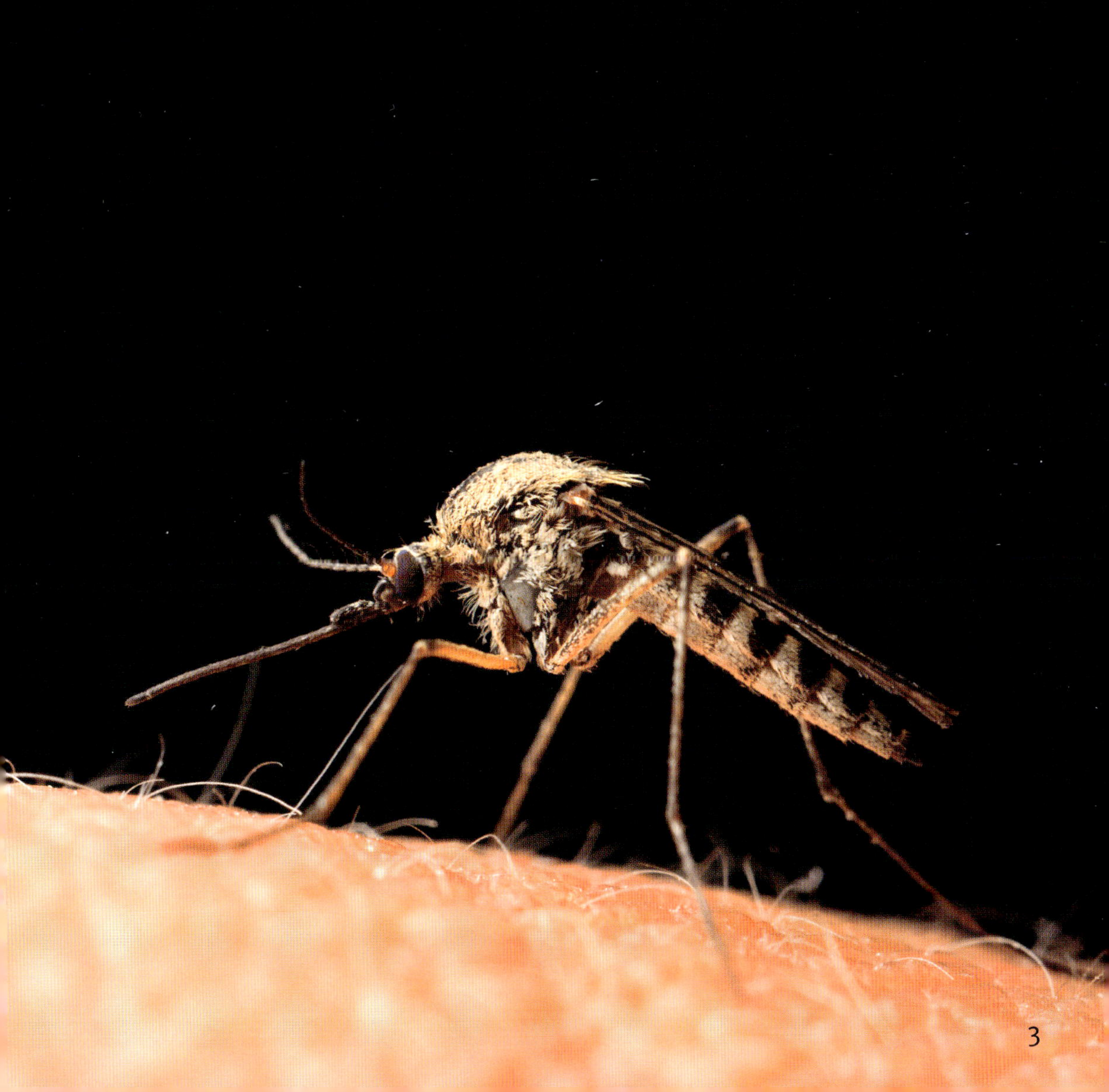

Flies and mosquitoes have six legs.
Their bodies are small, usually
between 1 and 7 millimetres long.
But there are some larger kinds of flies.

Flies have hairy bodies.
Their feet have pads and claws
that help them to cling to different surfaces
and land upside down on ceilings.

This robber fly is clinging to a leaf with its claws.

Mosquitoes have thin, **fragile** bodies and very long legs. They can land on flowers and other surfaces with the thin tips of their legs.

Most flies have soft, tube-like mouthparts for sucking up juices.

Mosquitoes have long, sharp tubes for pricking skin and sucking blood from animals and people.

Flies and mosquitoes smell food with their **antennae** (say: *an-ten-ee*). Their large **compound eyes** allow them to see movement in front or behind.

All insects have three main body parts: the head, the thorax and the abdomen.

Mosquitoes have large compound eyes.

Differences Between Flies and Mosquitoes

Flies	Mosquitoes
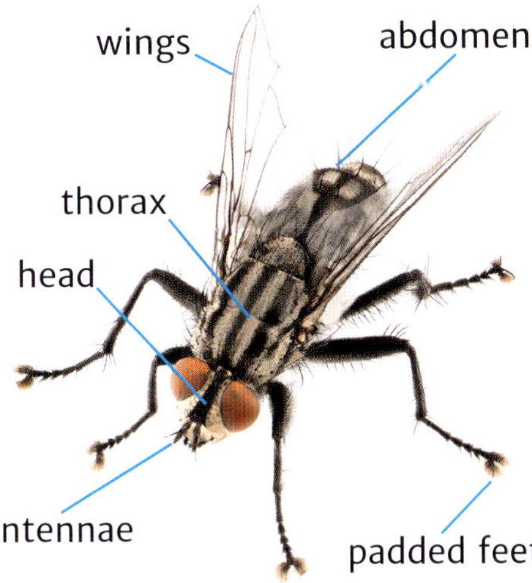 wings abdomen thorax head antennae padded feet	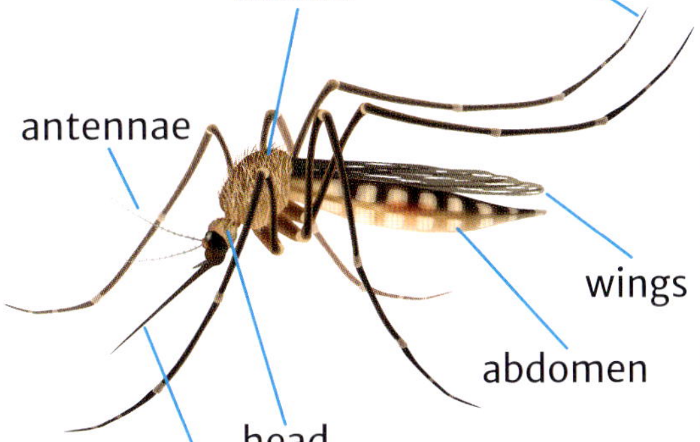 thin tips of legs thorax antennae wings abdomen head long mouthparts
mostly active during the day	mostly active in the evening and at night
small, hairy, sturdy body	thin, fragile body
hairy legs	long, thin legs
feet with pads and claws	thin tips of legs
rounded wings	narrow wings
short, stiff antennae	longer antennae
soft or sharp mouthparts	long, thin, sharp mouthparts

The Life Cycle of Flies and Mosquitoes

There are four **stages** in the life cycle of flies and mosquitoes.

Flies often lay their eggs in things that are soft and rotting, such as dead plants or **dung**. Mosquitoes lay eggs in water.

Wriggly grubs called larvae (say: *lar-vee*) hatch from the eggs and start eating the food around them. After the larva has eaten enough food, it forms a hard case around itself, called a pupa (say: *pyoo-pa*).

Inside the pupa, a larva's body changes.

An adult insect breaks out of the pupa, ready to fly.

Fly larvae are also called maggots.

The Life Cycle of a Mosquito

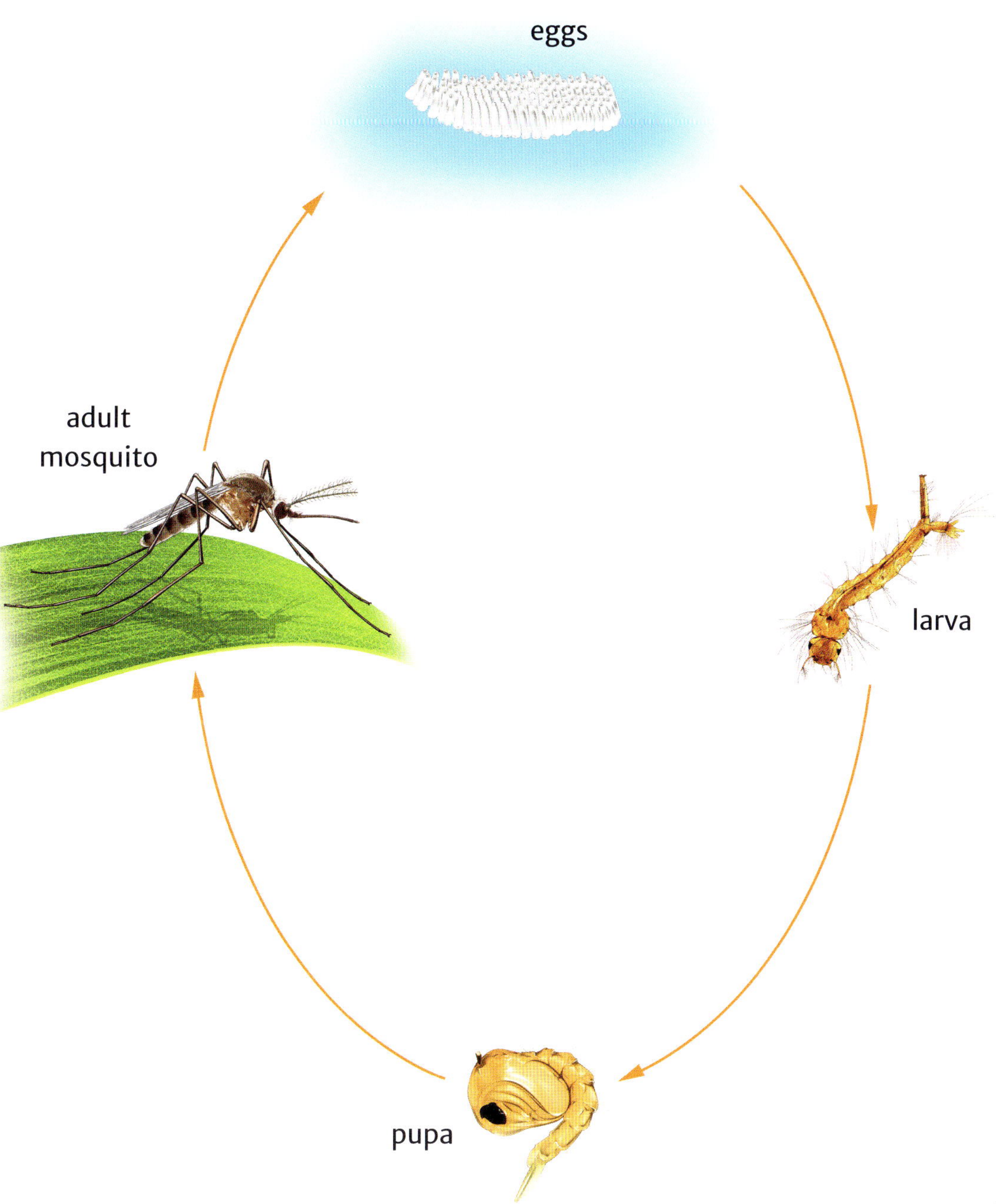

Where Flies and Mosquitoes Live

Flies can live almost anywhere on Earth, even in places covered in snow and ice.

Houseflies live near rubbish or compost bins, and near animals and their dung.

Yellow dung flies eat cow dung in a field.

Fruit flies live close to fruit and vegetables, such as on farms and in kitchens and gardens.

Many kinds of mosquitoes live in places with warm weather.
They stay close to water in **wetlands** and streams.

Mosquitoes often live in parks and gardens with ponds and bird baths. They can even lay their eggs in puddles!

These fruit flies are feeding on a cherry.

These mosquitoes live in a pond.

What Flies and Mosquitoes Eat

Most flies and mosquitoes cannot eat solid food.

Flies suck liquids from rotting plants and animals. They drink **nectar** from flowers. Flies also suck up liquids from food they find on people's plates.

This is a close-up photo of a housefly sucking up marmalade from a slice of toast.

It is only female mosquitoes that suck blood. They need the blood to make their eggs. Male mosquitoes use their long mouth tube to drink nectar from deep inside flowers.

This male mosquito is drinking the nectar from a flower.

Flying Skills

Flies have special flying skills.
They can quickly change direction in the air,
and even fly upside down.
They can also fly on windy days,
and some can **hover** in the air.

Flies have strong muscles for beating their wings at high speed.
Mosquitoes beat their wings even faster than flies.
The mosquitoes' wings make a buzzing sound.

Both flies and mosquitoes have strong muscles for steering their wings.
A tiny stalk, called a haltere (say: *hal-teer*), is behind each wing. The halteres are important for balance, and stop flies and mosquitoes from spinning out of control.

Different Kinds of Flies and Mosquitoes

Horseflies are large, slow-moving flies.
They often bite horses, other animals and people.
Their mouthparts are sharp enough
to prick crocodile skin.

This horsefly is biting a person's hand.

Hoverflies are colourful flies
that look almost the same as bees or wasps.
Unlike those insects, hoverflies cannot sting.

Birds can be tricked by a hoverfly's markings.
Most birds will not try to eat hoverflies
because the birds do not want to be stung.
Hoverflies can safely hover and dash between flowers,
feeding on nectar and **pollen**.

A bite from a mosquito usually gives a person an itchy, red lump.
But several kinds of dangerous mosquitoes do more harm than this.
Their bite can spread diseases.

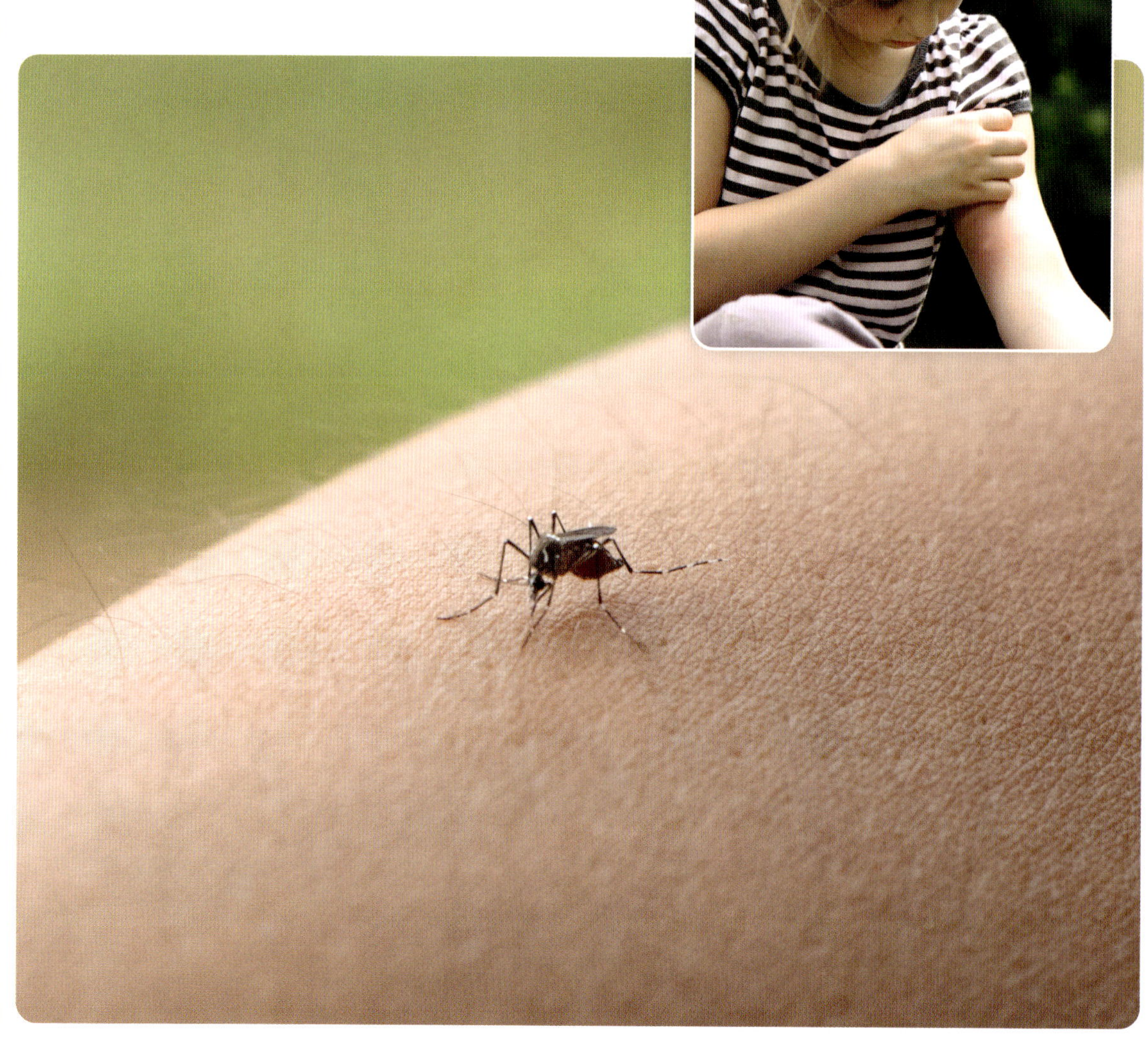

One of these diseases is malaria (say: *muh-lair-ree-uh*).
It only occurs in some parts of the world,
and can make people very sick.
Every year, many people die from malaria.

People can use insect spray or cover most of their bodies with clothing to prevent mosquito bites.

These people have covered their faces with nets to protect against mosquito bites.

Not Just Pests

Most people think flies and mosquitoes are pests.

Flies can spread thousands of tiny germs. They might land on rubbish, then fly away and land on someone's food!

Mosquitoes often bite people while they sleep, and some kinds of mosquitoes can spread disease.

These flies are feeding on someone's food.

However, flies and mosquitoes also do useful things. Some spread pollen in farmers' crops so that fruit and vegetables can grow. Some kinds of fly larvae eat caterpillars and small insects that could ruin crops.

Some flies and mosquitoes spread pollen, which helps crops like these avocados to grow.

These fly larvae are eating a caterpillar.

The larvae of flies and mosquitoes help to clean the environment by eating rotting animals and waste.

Many animals, such as birds, bats, spiders, reptiles and fish, eat flies and mosquitoes. Without these insects, the animals would have no food to eat.

Flies and mosquitoes are not just pests. They are an important part of life on Earth.

Glossary

antennae (*noun*) feelers or stalks on an insect's head

compound eyes (*noun*) eyes that are made up of different parts that work separately

dung (*noun*) solid waste from animals

fragile (*adjective*) not very strong; breaks easily

hover (*verb*) to stay in one place while in the air

nectar (*noun*) a sweet liquid made by flowers

pollen (*noun*) the powder that is found inside flowers, which helps to make new seeds

stages (*noun*) the separate parts of a process

wetlands (*noun*) land where there is a lot of water

Index